# SLEEPLESS

## A LOVE STORY

By

Eric Murphy

# SLEEPLESS

# CONTENTS

ACKNOWLEGDEMENT ............................................3

PREFACE....................................................... 4

CHAPTER 1: Sleepless/Ledgend .................................6

CHAPTER 2: Priceless/Cakes .................................... 40

CHAPTER3: Careless/Elise....................................52

CHAPTER 4: Fearless/Swift .....................................68

CHAPTER 5: Heartless/Gunz....................................74

CHAPTER 6: Reckless/Taylor ...................................78

CHAPTER 7: They Grow Up Too Fast........................ 91

CHAPTER 8: Like Looking in A Mirror.....................92

CHAPTER 9: Hope/Speechless ................................. 93

CHAPTER 10: One Hot Summer............................... 97

ABOUT THE AUTHOR ..........................................101

# ACKNOWLEGDEMENT

To my wife, Rosa Lina Murphy, thank you for
always standing by my side. Love you always.

To my son, Lucas Alexander Murphy, always follow
your dreams. Daddy loves you forever and always.

To my friends, Nicolas Flores and Sonya Warren,
thank you for always believing.

To Tianna Faminia, thank you for always telling me
to try and calling me a talented piece of shit, Lol!

# PREFACE

Growing up, I always felt out of place as a biracial teenager, half Irish and half Puerto Rican, with a few other influences peppered in. Reading opened me up to new worlds and perspectives in life. I couldn't find a book that told my story: a teenager trying to find his way in Red Hook, Brooklyn, a place that was always in the news, receiving a spotlight for drugs and murder. Red Hook was a neighborhood that most people would avoid.

But to me, it was home, the place that turned me into the man I am today. One day, while walking through coffee park, I had my first rap battle. During one of my shopping trips, I picked up a couple of bootleg hip-hop instrumental mixtapes and found an outlet to express myself by writing bars in a small notebook. I spent my nights listening to DJ Red Alert, and one night, he put on the new Slick Rick song "Children's Story " a song that told more of a story than a dance track. After hearing it on replay, I soon started writing storyboard hip-hop. Over the years, I perfected my craft and became known in music circles as "The Ledgend, "renowned for my storyboard hip-hop style.

After the death of my father, writing became my solace. He died when I was fifteen when I needed him the most. I started writing a narrative story known as "Sleepless" a story I wrote at night when I was kept up by my thoughts and processing my emotions. As a teenager, I began writing the urban narrative I yearned to read.

# CHAPTER 1

## Sleepless/Ledgend

### "Time is money, how long can you stay up?"

Time is money. The average person gets from six to eight hours of sleep a night and works about forty hours a week to come home with just enough to pay rent, eat a fast-food lunch, catch a movie once a month.

My name is Jacob. But everybody calls me Ledgend I never been the type to work a nine-to-five. To be honest with you I hustle make money, with my mind. Live on a constant grind, Talk. Like a boss walk with a swagger. Clean white tee fresh fitted brim low.

My jeans are the only true religion I know. Stay with that girl and that boy you want it I got everything you need Just don't ask where it came from.

It's three in the morning, and I just finished my last sip of Henny and red bull to chase the time. As I turn my phone pings. The first fiend of the night. I keep my eyes wide open as I walk. The block is hot like a topless bar even though its twenty below.

The boys are out playing peekaboo in the new Magnums, each holding about two magnums. I am about to make my first stop at the homie. Los's crib to get some work cut and processed.

When it comes to cutting Cocaine, Los is like a master chef. He can turn a brick of hard white into the perfect Beige. Adding just the right amount of sauce to keep the fiends coming back faithfully.

It's around 3:30 pm, I move about a brick in a half If everything goes right, I should be back by four, the block is looking real Resident Evil Flooded with zombies, I moved about six hits until I hear gunshots followed by sirens. Kind of funny how gunshots are always followed by sirens. When you live in the hood, barely surviving.

As I turn, my phone goes off. It's a text message from a shorty named Elise. I met in the park about a week ago. She sent me a message full of emojis.

I texted her, "What are you up to, love?" She replies, "Just chilling at home, watching TV. Bored as fuck." I asked, "Wanna smoke?" She responds, "Sure, text me your info. I'll be there in about five minutes. Just need to make a quick stop at the crib."

I head home, grab a can of Pepsi, slip two magnums into my pocket, put on a fresh white tee, and a pair of blue jeans, and slip on my new white and gray sevens. I also tuck a Thirty-Eight in my waist, just in case. You never know when you might need protection.

After a quick walk, I arrive at the Shorty's crib, 80 Dwight Street, apartment 5A. I reach out to knock but notice the door is open already, always a good sign.

As I walk in the door, I hear Taylor's latest single blasting from the speakers, as my phone goes off. The message reads, "I'm in my room, come in."

That's what's up...

I walk down a small hallway to a half-open door. I turn the knob and there she is, in a tight wife beater and Hello Kitty pajamas, looking both innocent and seductive at the same time. As we lay in bed, I toss two dubs out as she pulls out four vanilla Dutches from her dresser drawer.

My kind of girl.

I reach out for a CD to break up, on and see the new Taylor album on her dresser. Before I can open it, she snatches it from my hands. "That's my boo," she says with a sexy little giggle.

The bud rolls two fat boys and two models skinny as fuck. With every pull, the room becomes more of a blur. Everything but the angel in front of me. Her eyes glisten a cross of blue and green under the blinking fluorescents.

I am lost in them only for a second, then she hits me square in the face with a pillow. "What are you looking at?" she says as she meets my lips with a planned kiss. She quickly strips down to her panties. They are the perfect accent to her silhouette: white lace with a pink bow. What can I say? I'm into details.

I kissed my way down from her neck to her stomach, taking her panties down with my teeth.   Her scent was mesmerizing, she got on top of me  and began to ride me. Like a wave with the skill of a surfer so tight and wet, I must be dreaming.

She took me in even though the pain showed in her eyes, I grabbed her by the hips and turned her over on her back as her feet rested on my shoulders. She was on her second orgasm before.

I realized I forgot to use protection. At this point, I didn't even care, her moans motivated me to go harder until I couldn't hold back any longer. After a quick kiss on the cheek, I got dressed as Elise slept with "Tears on Her Pillow" playing in the background.

I checked the time on my phone, it was 4:20 pm. I laughed to myself, remembering the old saying, "Even a broken clock is right twice a day."

I walked to the corner store and ordered a small black coffee with three sugars. Downing it like a can of soda, I headed towards the Ave, the sound of sirens and cop cars filled the air. I turned the corner too quickly to turn back.

I couldn't tell if it was the bud or the lack of sleep that had me paranoid. Ever get that feeling like you're being watched? I kept a brisk pace all the way home, deciding to call it a night after a warm shower.

I slipped into a fresh white tee and hit the sack. I ate some leftover General Tao's chicken from the night before. For some reason, I couldn't sleep, my heart beating a mile a minute. No matter how I turned, I could hear it pounding like an echo in my ears.

I stood up the whole night pacing the floor of my apartment, watching the red light of my alarm clock. Time seemed to move so fast. The next thing I knew it was morning. I went to the bathroom and saw the scratches on my back, a reminder of the night before.

I turned to my sink to wash my face then looked in the mirror, my eyes were bloodshot and black, but I was wide awake. I stood in the crib for about an hour then hit the block to catch the afternoon rush of fiends on their way back from the methadone center.I moved about a bundle as my stomach began to rumble in hunger, I took a slow walk to the chicken spot.

As the boys drove by. Fuck! I hope they don't stop me. I walked inside the chicken spot as they circled the block like vultures.

Then I saw her, my angel, Elise. God knows I needed one right now she pulled me close to her and whispered in my ear, "Here comes the boys." Then she pulled me forward, wrapped her arms around me, and gave me a passionate kiss while she probed my pockets and then walked away with a wink. The boys came in a second later and took me outside for a search but found nothing on me.

I love that girl.

As I walked home, I received a text from her with a smile I replied, "See you later, I love you." Yeah, I said it. The only difference was that I meant it this time. I never thought I would fall for her so fast. She was supposed to be a hit and run, we ended up playing tag and she was it.

Every day, we touched base and spent most of our time together, our nights in bed, usually at my place. The sex was crazy, there was never a dull moment. She definitely is not the reason I haven't slept in days.

I felt like I was living in a daze ahead of time, moving fast but getting nowhere. My eyes showed tiredness but were wide open. The smallest things seem amazing to me, like watching the sunset and rising with the one I love. I didn't see the need to get high anymore.

I just felt dizzy, I tried popping an E pill. I tripped and almost broke my arm on the way down. Even when I fail, she's always there for me by my side my angel Elise. It's been about two weeks since I last slept. I called Elise, but all I get is her answering machine.

As an attempt to tire myself out, I head to the park basketball courts to play a couple of games of ball. It's the perfect day for a ball game, cloudy atmosphere with a light breeze as I walk through the park, with my eyes wide open.

I turned my head slowly to scan who was on the court when suddenly I got hit with a roundhouse punch to my jaw.
I stumbled, took a few steps back, and shook the cobwebs out of my head.

As I hear the words that killed me on the inside, "You are fucking my sister, she is only fifteen," followed by another swing. I quickly ducked this one and responded back with a two-piece, and a hook from left field. When the punch connected; it sounded like a gunshot. I had a lot of questions for scrap, but he was out cold. I was out of the park before the sirens got closer.

As I walked to my crib, I got a text from Elise, "I really don't know how to tell you this, but I'm fifteen, I thought you knew and I'm pregnant and keeping the baby.
I'm sorry about my brother, we need to talk."


Damn, now I know how Usher felt.

I quickly got tired of the phone games and walked down to Elise's building. As I enter the door, I see Elise posted up with some pretty boy, exchanging numbers. I pulled my hoodie up as I walked by and straight cold-cocked him.

I looked back as he fell asleep in Elise's arms. I turned back and looked Elise in the eyes with the look of death, she had no response for me just tears. As I walked away heartbroken, I said to myself, "The only one I loved played me. I thought you were different. Fuck love, it's time to hit the block."

It's been a week, and a few young boys are trying to take my place. I post up in the mailbox, waiting for trouble to come my way. With the mood that I am in, I welcome it. I stand and wait, hoodie up, brim low, hand on my hammer, finger on the trigger. A young scrap came up to me and reached out for a pound. "Where have you been?" I responded,

"Everywhere," with my hand on the hammer the whole time. After some small talk, I realized it was my homie Gun's cousin Swift. Before I could say a word, Swift began to speak, "My cousin told me to see you about some work. You have been missing in action for a minute. Me and my people got the customers, we heard you're the man to speak to. I got you, but everything comes through me. A fifty split down the middle."

"How many workers you got?" I inquired. "Two," he replies, "My scrap ace and my cousin Franklin. As long as we stay small, we can make that paper." Swift is driven, but I don't trust him. There's something about the look in his eyes. I will keep him close, put him under my wing, and if he tries to fly, clip him.

It's been about a week, and business is metro booming. Got that boy and that girl on deck, and half the hood under my control. I was bringing in so much paper, but I'm not happy. Every day, I grow more paranoid.

Ever feel like something bad is about to go down? Just don't know what, when, or even why. Maybe, I'm just bugging, but I was going to see Swift anyway to see what he has been up to and get my cut of this month's profits. As I walked out of my building, to the sound of light raindrops on the pavement, I got about a block away and heard a gun cock in my ear.

Followed by a freeze, before I could put my hands up, I was thrown up against the hood of a parked car. I got searched, but they found nothing on me. I felt like I could be arrested any minute today. Luck was on my side; if they had waited a few more minutes, I would have been on a long bus trip to Rikers.

I headed back to my crib after stopping for a couple of slices of pizza. Once I got home, I stripped down and looked in the mirror, but I don't recognize myself. I have lost about twenty pounds in three weeks. I jumped in the shower, and the water "was ice cold, an amazing start to the day."

I called Swift and told him to lay low for a while. It was time for a change. I had been grinding my whole life and had nothing to show for it except a couple of pairs of sneakers and some gear. I needed to move up in this world, make a fresh start, and go big one last time.

After texting for a few weeks, Elise and I moved into a new place in the city about an hour away. After moving in, I called Los to meet me halfway. I bought two G- packs of ecstasy and two bricks of cocaine at a decent price. I taped the work to my waist and hopped on the Atrain express. In about an hour, I was home, just in time to beat a storm as I walked in the door.

I saw my girl's cousin, Cakes, asleep on the sofa. Elise called me to the bedroom and told me the deal: her cousin was going to be staying with us for a while until she got back on her feet.

Things were finally falling into place. I needed a cute girl to hit the clubs with, and with Elise expecting, she wasn't up for it. But Cakes was ready and willing to work for a small cut and a place to stay, and I can't knock her hustle.

We decided to hit the clubs that weekend to make some moves and line up some customers. Cakes played the role of hook-up, sitting at the bar waiting for a few guys to flirt with her. She would ask if they wanted to party, call me over, and then we' make some sales.

I ground my teeth as we waited in line for the first of many clubs. I paid the bouncer and walked in through the VIP entrance like a Rockstar, playing the background while Cakes worked the room like a game of chess.

After about an hour, we hit the next club. By four, the clubs were closed. Half the work had been moved, and I was feeling nice off Grey Goose and cranberry.

Cakes was twisted. We took a cab home and stumbled through the door. Elise had left a note for me, "Hey babe, went to stay over Mom's for the night. See you tomorrow. There's some food in the fridge." Cakes kicked off her shoes and sat on the couch. I reached in for a kiss on the cheek but got a kiss on the lips.

I stood in awe as her dress hit the floor.

Why do wrong things feel so right?

I grabbed her by the hips and threw Cakes up against the wall. Our bodies met in rough strokes every now and then. Pausing to take breaths after her first orgasm, I let her down slowly.

With a naughty look in her eyes, she grabbed me by the hand and led me towards the shower. I began to bite my way down her neck to the small star tattoo on her midriff. She quickly pushed me against the wall and began to ride me.

The look in her eyes was so intoxicating that within a few strokes, I came inside her. I stood in the shower shocked and disappointed in myself, but what was done was done. There was no turning back now, and I looked forward to taking the ride.

The next day, Elise walked in on me and Cakes playing Wii bowling. We tried to act natural. After a quick lunch, I took the F train to surprise Swift. It had been about a week since I hit the hood, and I needed to clear my mind.

As I got off the train, it began to snow. I stuck out my tongue, catching a flake, a chill ran through my body. I started walking, noticing a black van with tinted windows following me. I quickened my pace, cutting through the park, but the van remained on my trail. As I Reaching my block, I saw the van stop. Swift came running toward me.

with urgency in his stride. Suddenly, the van door slid open, and two goons dressed in black jumped out, brandishing shotguns. Before I could pull my hammer, shots rang out. Swift was hit twice and fell to the ground. The van sped off, blaring

The new Taylor single, ''Shots Fired' 'as it disappeared into the snowy night. As I held Swift in my arms, his body grew cold. His breath thinned by the minute, but I couldn't stop it. Looking down, I saw a blank look in his eyes Swift was dead. I ran home, threw my clothes in the incinerator, and took a shower. As blood dripped from my hands, I couldn't help but feel responsible.

I got dressed as my phone went off. It was Gunz, Swift's cousin. He had heard about Swift and wanted payback an eye for an eye, a body for a body. I dressed in all black, strapped on two guns, and headed to the train. Just then, an Escalade pulled up. The window rolled down, and there was Taylor. He gave me a head nod, a smirk, and a wink.

As I looked down, I noticed Taylor had a fraction in his lap. Before I could reach him, a cop car pulled up behind us. I shot Taylor a look of pure rage before descending into the train station. Anger consumed me as I grappled with Swift's death and the looming threat on my own life. I had been laying low since his murder, avoiding the streets where danger lurked.

Each passing day meant more lost income, but I knew that I couldn't hide forever. The time had come to confront the source of my troubles before it consumed me entirely.

Word on the street was that Taylor had a performance at the Tunnel a club in the city. I pulled some strings and managed to gain access through the back door. Inside, I spotted Cakes, who had caught Taylor's attention. I laughed to myself as I watched her flirt with him, knowing that she was about to play a crucial role in my plan.

"She offered him a drink, and" as he leaned in for a kiss, she discreetly slipped a roofie into his glass. An hour later, she led him to the bathroom, unwittingly walking him into my trap.

my hands shook as I waited in the next door stall. It was too late to turn back now. I opened the stall door and fired two shots into Taylor's chest. Then, I pulled the fire alarm on my way out, sending the club into a full-blown panic.

Weaving through the frantic crowd, I held Cakes by the arm. We jumped into the first cab we saw. As we pulled away, the wail of sirens pierced the night as an ambulance sped past us. I reached over and pulled Cakes' close, trying to keep it all together.

Taylor survived the shooting. Gunz took over where Swift left off. Since that night, Cakes and I haven't spoken. Out of both need and guilt, I gave Gunz all my leftover work and Swift's cut. As I got home,

I heard Elise scream her water had broken.

The baby was coming. They say when someone dies, a new life takes their place on earth. After fourteen hours, the baby was born. It was a girl, and we named her Hope. She became the reason to write a new chapter for my family.

It had been a month since I last slept, and I feared I was losing my mind. Time was slipping away from me, but today was a good day. It was time to see my child, but first, I needed a fresh cut.

I hopped off the F train at Ninth Street to get a cut from Henry, a man who had been cutting hair since before I was born. After waiting what seemed like an hour, it was my turn. As I sat in the barber's chair, the whole room started spinning.

I didn't notice the man in the mirror in front of me. Every time the clippers touched my hair, my skin crawled. Even though I knew I was in good hands, something felt off. After twenty minutes, I was done. I got up from the barber chair, but everything was a blur.

the next thing I knew, I was picking myself up from the floor. I turned, saw myself in the mirror, and let out a scream. With a roundhouse punch, the glass shattered, and I was covered in my own blood. I threw a large knot of money out my pocket,

But I couldn't stop I had somewhere to be.

My baby and wife needed me. As I walked into the hospital, everyone stared at me. I felt myself breaking down. They were coming to take me away, but I wasn't going without a fight.

I knocked out a doctor and punched a nurse in the ribs. A sharp pain shot through my shoulder, and I woke up in a small room with no shoelaces. I got up, dragging my body down a long hallway, driven by an unexplainable urge to know where it led.

I reached a desk and was greeted with a warm hello from a nurse named Paula. "Welcome to Six South," she said. "If you need anything, I'm here all night.

I sat on a large white couch, my legs crossed, and time seemed to move so slow. Every now and then, other patients paced up and down the hallway, laughing at jokes in their heads, that they only knew the punchlines too. Only if they knew this was not a happy place, and I couldn't leave. The doors were closed, and I needed space some room to breathe. I headed back to my room to sit and think.

I closed the door to rest, hoping the room would stop spinning. Just as I lay down there was a knock at the door .it was a doctor named mike holding a small cup of pills: one blue, one red and a half of a white one. He said the pills would help me stay calm and relax. I refused to take them.

About an hour passed, and I felt like a puppet being pulled by strings, but I wasn't in control of myself. I walked up to mike and asked for the pills, took them and walked back to my room.

"The next thing I knew, there was a knock on the "door around eight-thirty in the morning. It was time to wake up. I had never been up this early in my life. My head and body hurt, but I felt more in control.

I headed to the front desk, holding the wall the whole way. My legs felt so heavy, my body so light. I looked in the mirror my eyes were huge, fully dilated. In other words, I was fucking high.

My vision blurred, and the next thing I knew, I was covered in cold sweat. The whole room was looking at me in shock. I had fallen straight on my face. I knew this from the pain in my head and shoulder.

I later found out that the reason I passed out was low blood pressure, a result of not eating for three days. Everyone around me seemed crazy.

I can't take "this place. I couldn't even watch TV without seeing someone rocking, laughing, or talking to their imaginary friend, who, by the way, was a whore. The guy next door to me just screamed all day behind a closed door. Fighting his own personal demons.

After breakfast, I was met by a short, sexy doctor named Jenn. She said I had a nervous breakdown but assured me I was in good hands. She told me my wife and daughter were doing fine and that Elise would come to see me tomorrow. I hated the thought of her seeing me like this, but if I denied her visit, it would crush her.

So, I have to play the role, and put on a mask for the one I loved. My leg began to shake as I sat and looked out a large window onto the street. As it began to snow. The cold outside slowly fogged the glass. All my life, I had never taken the time to watch, snow fall it was so relaxing.

"People say every snowflake is different, no two are" alike. I'm lucky I have two snowflakes in my life: Cakes, the object of my desire, and Elise, my best friend and lover.

The nurse told me I had company as I drew faces on the window. I turned my head and saw Cakes, looking amazing but so sad. I asked if she was okay, and she responded, "I'm okay, just late." Before I could say I wasn't expecting her to visit, she kissed my cheek and whispered in my ear,

"I'm not sure, but I might be pregnant."

Couldn't she start with, "Hi, I miss you, "

I'm bringing life into this world and losing myself at the same time. I pulled up a seat next to Cakes and watched the snow as it slowly fell while she rested her head on my shoulder. Times like this made me wish time could just stand still, but time kept moving.

"At eight-thirty, visiting hours were about to be over "for the night. Cakes took off her name ring and put it on my thumb. We went to my room and shared a quick kiss behind closed doors. I spent most of my day in the TV room watching a Loony Tunes marathon.

With a room full of nuts, I felt more like an M&M a nut with a thick shell. Everybody around me was off the wall nuts. Tony was acting out Frank White again; it was becoming routine. It was time for a walk.

As I strolled, I noticed there was a new guy in my wing named Ben. Last night, he was off the chain, but today he seemed cool. It was always interesting meeting new faces in this place.

The doctors said we had to interact, so I asked Ben to get two other people to play Monopoly. In a place like this you need to build a circle around you. Monopoly was a good way to see who you could trust.

"Later in the night, a new girl named Eve was brought in, a Russian Shorty who looked so beautiful and so tired. After chilling for a day, I invited her to play. Even though she was overly drugged, she decided to join us.

Eve picks the dog because it reminded her of her dog Bear. Ben picked the money bag because he was a paper chaser. I picked the car because I like the fast lane. The game ran slow, and for once I was at ease. After passing around war stories, we all decided to go to bed, I passed out faster than a fiend could sell Christmas toys.

I woke up to a knock at my door around twelve. It's was Elise she leaned in for a hug. I turned cakes name ring around hoping she didn't notice. Elise looked beautiful but not herself. She had never been good at hiding her pain.

She is like an open book, but she was my favorite novel. We spent the whole day together, just cuddled up and talking on the big white couch I had made my home base. Just as we were ready to kiss, a doctor walked up to us and said I needed to get some tests done, a CAT scan. There was something I needed to drink for the X-rays to show better; it tasted like lemonade mixed with salt.

Elise had papers to fill out, and after a long hug, she left but promised to be back tomorrow. I finally drank the nasty lemonade; it was time for the test. I was brought downstairs in a wheelchair by a Debo male nurse. He took me through a set of doors to a small room with a machine straight out of Frankenstein.

I was quickly put on a table, and I felt a hot pinch in my arm where they stuck an IV tube. A mask was put over my head, more like a cage around my face. A hot rush flowed through my body from my head to my toes; I felt hot, then cold rushes.

I stared at the ceiling as a red dot floated in front of my face. It sounded like I was in a jet engine. I closed my eyes to keep a handle on my nerves. It felt like my world was shaking.

Then it was over. I stood up, and my legs felt heavy, and I was incredibly dizzy. I hadn't eaten lunch since I had to do the test on an empty stomach. I was brought upstairs in a wheelchair, like a dog on a leash.

I went to my room and wrote down the day's events on a calendar that Elise had brought me a week ago. It was time for me to rest. After a half- hour nap, I was on my feet just in time for lunch. I met Ben and Eve in the hallway,

we walked to lunch together. Eve looked more upbeat today and told me about a music class at two. I told her I'd go only if she danced with me. She shot me a look and a cute smile as she walked by. After a quick lunch of dry rice and chicken wings, I turned my head to look at the TV. The news at noon reported that Gunz and Franklin had been caught up in a big drug bust in the hood. Los' crib had been raided. I guessed today was my lucky day; if I were on the outside, "I'd be knocked. "Right now.

Better them than me. I had to get myself right and my life straight. The room quickly emptied. All the tables were put up against the walls, and the chairs were moved to form a circle. An iPod was hooked up to a stereo system. Just as I was about to leave, Eve walked in, so I stayed. There were cookies and hot drinks.

I could go for a cookie, or three, as Eve sat in a chair sipping her chocolate like a shy girl at the club. I laughed to myself. What was a girl like her doing in a place like this? I guess we all had our issues.

Eve jumped up to the latest Reggaeton song and began to dance like she was in a trance. The music had a hold on her, but she was in charge, winding her hips like a gypsy. Her green eyes looked so innocent. I got up to dance with her. If we were in a club, it would be on, but I stayed well behaved and kept my distance.

"As we began to battle, the whole room's eyes were on us. "I hadn't danced like this in years. I didn't know if it was the meds or a small piece of me coming back. Eve and I became fast homies. Ben was like my right hand. I went to my room, where I was met by the head psychiatrist.

He said the scan came out clear.

"Guess I'm just crazy then, huh?" I responded.

He quickly said, "Not crazy. You just had a small breakdown." Sometimes your life moves so fast that you need time for your mind to catch up.

In a few days, I should be going home. Elise hasn't seen me in days. I'm starting to worry even though I'm trying hard not to let it show. Maybe something came up.

I hope the baby's okay.

Then I got a knock on the door from Cakes. We went for a walk, and she told me everything was gone. Money was low, and Elise had moved back in with her mom. But she was coming tomorrow to take me home.

I gave Cakes back her ring with a kiss on the cheek. It was over between us. The next day finally came, and the doctors said it was my day to go.

I was given a pill case and a time chart for my meds. Elise brought me my red Champion hoodie, blue jeans, and a pair of Timberland boots.

I ate my final lunch with Eve and Ben. It was hard to say goodbye, but we exchanged numbers and planned to meet on the outside. After lunch, I was met by Elise and my daughter, Hope.

I headed to the elevator, trying not to look back. Eve ran to me and gave me a big hug and a kiss on the cheek. Elise rolled her eyes but knew the deal and kept moving. As I walked outside, it began to snow.

"I stood for a minute as the cold air hit me, taking in everything around me. You never know what you've got till it's gone.

Even the small things seemed like "the world to me.

Time is money how long can you stay up?
And what's money if you never enjoy life?

I walked into Elise's crib. Cakes' eyes were full of tears. Elise and Cakes headed into the bathroom you could hear a pin drop, followed by Elise saying, "Why can't you tell me who the father is?"

I sat on the couch holding Hope in my arms, watching the real world, not knowing mine was about to fall apart. Cakes headed for the door and threw something at my feet.

It was a pregnancy test. As I looked down and saw a small plus on it, she turned to Elise and said, "I'm sorry," then walked out the door. I headed out the door to follow, and then it happened my life ended in a single shot. I lay there as my body grew cold. My life flashed before my eyes, and I fell fast asleep.

**"Some say money is the root of all evil. Time is money, and life is short. Live every day like it's your last because it just might be."**

# CHAPTER 2

## Priceless/Cakes

" Love is blind, caring, and kind. Real love is hard to find. Love will make you lose your mind. Love is a battlefield."

My name is Katelyn, but everybody calls me Cakes. A guy once told me, "God must love you because you have a body that's a blessing."

I never thought. I would ever fall in love until I met him. I don't know if it was his swagger or the way he moved that got me open on a different level.

What am I saying? He's my cousin Elise's man. About a week has passed since my ex laid hands on me. Thank God for butcher knives. I've been crashing at my cousin's place, mostly just kicking it on the couch watching Netflix. I need to get this bread up "so I can get a place of my own."

My cousin's man, Jacob, asked me to help him with business. We have been moving Cocaine and Ecstasy every night, dancing under the dim lights of every club in this city. He's so fly. What am I saying? He barely looks my way. His eyes tease me with every glance.

Tonight's the night Elise is staying over at my Aunt Julie's for some mother-daughter time. I put on my new black dress, a push-up bra, a pair of black heels, and hazel contacts. I left my hair wild, just begging to be pulled.

I was getting hot just thinking about it. We left around ten and started hitting clubs everywhere we went. We got VIP treatment. I laughed as eyes rolled while we passed every line and just walked through the front door.

Jacob was looking right tonight, but I couldn't concentrate on him now. I had a job to do take a seat at the bar and play the shy role, just waiting for a guy to show interest. I could spot a coke head from a mile away.

These days my job was simple: see a dude, get him to buy, wink at Jacob behind my shoulder to bring me the merchandise, take the money, and then, when things got too hot, leave.

At the next club, the night was kind of slow. I drank a Long Island iced tea, and Jacob had a double shot of Patron. I asked him to dance. He resisted at first, but after some puppy dog eyes, he gave in. I began to slowly grind his waist; I could tell he was getting excited. I laughed to myself as he tried to play it off.

It was 4 am, and all the clubs were starting to close. It wasn't hard to tell we were both wasted; the Red Bull shots had me wide awake. We stumbled as we walked up the steps to his place, holding each other up as we walked through the door.

We both landed on the couch, tired from the night's work. I wanted to stay up tonight. I leaned in and kissed his lips. At first, he didn't react, but quickly we began to French kiss like catching fish in a barrel. I took a deep sigh and took my panties off.

How could something so wrong feel so right?

I quickly stripped into my birthday suit and grabbed him by the hand. The way he was kissing down my body drove me crazy, from my neck to my midriff. I started to moan heavily as he licked my fresh star tattoo, still red from the day before.

My body began to twitch with every twist of his tongue. He was playing me like a violin, hitting all the right strings. My nipples grew hard as the cold water from the shower hit my body. I grabbed him by the neck as we kissed, slowly turning around so my knees wouldn't buckle. Each thrust felt like ecstasy, a mix of pleasure and pain

I didn't want it to stop, but with one last thrust, it was over. We both cleaned each other, sharing a body sponge. I stayed in the shower for a while, then took his t-shirt off the sink, put it on, and fell fast asleep. The next day, I woke up early and fixed breakfast scrambled eggs and burnt toast.

Elise walked in as I was whipping his ass in Wii bowling. She walked by without even a kiss; I guess she didn't know what she had. I put on some pink sweats, took my share of the profit money, plus a little extra, and hopped in a cab to the city to go shopping. I made the final down payment on a name ring I had on lay away, copped two pairs of the new Sevens, and headed to Red Hook to see my homie Jay and smoke a couple of blunts.

He had that fire haze; today was my lucky day. I turned my head and saw my ex posted up with the next chick. I walked by with an extra switch in my step and gave him a wink.

"I laughed to myself as his" jaw dropped when I walked away, laughing my ass off. I ate a slice of pizza and felt so dizzy I could almost pass out. I felt like I could throw up at any minute.

I hadn't seen my friend this month the one friend you hope never comes late. I took a few nights off to get some rest. Every day, I wore a mask in front of Elise, when the sun falls, I'm his and he's mine not in mind, but in body. Jacob had been acting strange lately and was on edge.

I asked if he was alright, and he said yes.

His eyes told another story; he hadn't been the same since Swift's death. But tonight was the night to make things right. We walked in through the back door after slipping the bouncer a dub. I saw Taylor at the bar, such a cocky fucker, throwing money around like it was new. You can't take the hood out of a nigga. After some small talk, I slipped a roffie into his drink.

A few moments later, he was done for. I led him into the bathroom with a false promise of things to come. If he only knew what was next.

I turned my head and saw Jacob Walk out of a stall in a ski mask, holding a gun. I turned around as shots were fired and headed to the next stall, beginning to hurl as Taylor slipped away. I pulled the fire alarm as we walked out through all the chaos. I felt lost, then I felt a hand pull me into a cab.

It was Jacob. I cried on his shoulder, dumb founded at what I had just taken part in. But what's done is done. I held his hand as he began to shake and kissed him on the cheek, and I fell asleep in his arms.

The next day I woke up with a killer headache. Everything began to spin as I threw up into the bathroom sink. I made an appointment with my doctor for Wednesday afternoon. It had been about a week since I last had my period. I turned on the television. The news was full of reports about "Taylor's shooting."

I walked outside like I was hiding from the paparazzi, wearing sunglasses and keeping my face covered. I got my hair cut short and wore a headscarf like Mary J. Blige or Lil' Kim.

Got it going on What... what?

I moved out of Elise's crib to my own place out of both need and guilt. I couldn't take the lies anymore. I spent the last two days in bed. I felt so tired no matter how much I slept, it wasn't enough.

After a long, warm shower, I bundled up and called a cab to the doctor's office. As I walked into the hospital, I saw Jacob fighting with two guards. I jumped in front of him as a nurse gave him a shot.

He soon passed out cold and was put on a stretcher and brought into the elevator. I went to my doctor, the whole time thinking about Jacob. I took a blood and urine test. I hate having to pee in those little cups; "I never know how much is enough, lol."

I left the doctor my cell number and ran down three flights of steps to the front desk to ask about Jacob. I almost slipped up and said I was his wife but caught myself and said I was Katelyn, his sister in law.

They told me he was in Six South, being admitted. I called Elise and told her I was going up to see him and to get some rest. Yeah, I can play the dumb role well. The receptionist told me I could see him in the morning.

I spent the night in the waiting room, sound asleep on the couch. A nurse handed me a blanket so I wouldn't catch a cold. I woke up the next day at seven like clockwork and went to the bathroom to wash my face. The cold water sent a chill up my spine.

After some cafeteria coffee, I got a visitor's pass. The elevator seemed to take forever; I wished it ran express. After a check of my bag, I was let in to see Jacob sitting at a window, watching the snowfall.

I nearly broke down into tears but played the tough role and headed his way. I grabbed him by the hand, covering up my tears with a quick wipe of a tissue. I passed him my ring, the only thing I had of my own, a meaningless token of success.

We talked for what seemed like hours. They say you never know love until it tests you. I hugged Jacob and said goodbye, not wanting to let go even though I knew deep down in my heart that he would never be mine.

I headed home and called Elise to tell her the news. I told her I would watch the baby so she could go see Jacob. Hope is beautiful; she has her father's eyes. After about an hour of Barney, Hope fell fast asleep.

I sat on the couch under a blanket, holding her and crying. I don't ever remember crying in my life. I went to the bathroom to wash my face and found a pregnancy test in the medicine cabinet. My leg shook as I took the test every time I get nervous, I turn into Thumper, lol.

I paced the bathroom floor; I didn't hear the door open it was Elise. I tried to hide the test, but it was too late. She had already seen the result. She began to ask me questions. I pushed her aside and walked toward the door, forgetting all about Jacob coming home today. In my frustration, I threw the test at his feet.

I stormed out, slamming the door behind me. I ran down the stairs at full speed, almost tripping on the way down. Jacob grabbed my arm to talk, but I pushed him away. He gave my ring back. He had already made his choice. I turned the corner, trying not to look back.

Suddenly, I heard a gunshot, which stopped me in my tracks. I turned around and saw Jacob lying in a pool of blood. I turned and said,

"I love you," but it was too late.

" You never know what you've got till it's gone. love is blind, caring, and kind. Love is a battlefield, and war never ends without "casualties. If you are brought down enough, you learn to defy gravity. I still ask God every day, is this how it had to be?"

# CHAPTER3

## Careless/Elise

**" When something feels right, it can't be wrong. When you fall in love, It's like a song. You never know what you got until it's gone."**

I still remember the first day I met Jacob in the park. It was my niece Jasmine's birthday, and the whole family was having a barbecue. I was on a swing, wasted when he passed by. The look in his eyes had me hooked. I swung back, and the next thing I knew, I was on the ground, and there he was with a handout, asking if I was okay. He helped me up, and I asked him his name.

"Jacob," he replied, but everybody called him Ledgend. After some small talk, we exchanged numbers. After a quick hug, he was gone. He stole my heart like a thief in the night. I couldn't get him off my mind; the thought of him turned me on.

About a week later, I hit him up with just a simple smile text. My mom and dad were gone for the night, my brother was out at the clubs with his boys, and I was bored out of my mind. So stressed from school, I needed some me time him and me time, I invited him over to smoke.

I had just broken up with my ex about a week ago, and I needed some sexual healing. I put on the tightest top I could find, a wife beater from my little brother's drawer, and my favorite Hello Kitty pajama bottoms.

I wore a Victoria's Secret set I had bought on the low for special times like this and put on the new Taylor single, "I'M SO IN LOVE" as high as it could go, I left the door open and waited for what seemed like a lifetime. Then I heard the door. The sound of his footsteps on my floor drove me crazy.

I sent him a text that I was in my room.

"As he walked in, my heart began to beat a mile a minute. I couldn't believe this was happening. I had" to calm down; we hadn't even started, and I was already all worked up.

I asked if he brought bud, and he laid on my bed and threw two dubs down like it was nothing to him. What can I say? I've always loved the hood type. Then he got a little crazy and tried to break up the bud on my new Taylor CD. Before he could open it, I snatched it away. "That's my boo," I said, laughing. He took a twenty out of his pocket and broke up on it instead.

The bud rolled two fat boys and two models skinny as fuck. We both took a blunt to the head and then had a small cipher with the other two. I turned my fan on to blow out the smoke, my room looking like London.

We looked into each other's eyes for what seemed like forever. Then I made a move and hit him with a pillow. The next thing I knew, my room was full of feathers.

"We fell back in bed as I kissed "his lips, and it was on. I quickly stripped down to my Vikki's as he began to kiss his way down to my midriff, taking my panties down with his teeth and tugging on them like a bad puppy but then he took control and began to eat me out like he had been fasting, and I was his first meal.

Every time his tongue hit my clit; I was on fire, damn!. I love older men, they get it in, not like the boys in high school. He got more swagger than anyone I ever fucked with.

Plus, he got a big dick it barely fit inside me but did. It felt amazing, the first thrust sent a shiver up my spine, I was coming closer to a climax with every stroke. I rolled over on him, it's my time to be on top. I rode him slow, taking in as much as I could and when he was in, I went wild.

I'm keeping this one if he doesn't kill me first. I hopped off and bent over, he grabbed my legs, lifted them up, and hit spots that I didn't even know I had. We were in perfect sync.

"Matching my moans with every stroke, I wanted "more but my body couldn't take it anymore. With one last thrust, I let go and had the best orgasm of my life, but it wasn't over. He picked me up and laid me on the bed like a priceless gift and ended with a slow thrust and a final kiss, and the next thing I knew it was morning.

Damn, he had put me to bed. The next day, I took a shower and was uber hungry, craving chicken as I walked to the chicken spot. There he was, my baby, buying a slice of pizza. The block was hot today, the boys kept making rounds. Damn, all I needed was to lose this guy to the system. I crossed the street.

I whispered in his ear, "Here come the boys," as I quickly picked his pockets while we shared a passionate kiss. I walked out just as the boys walked in. After a few minutes, I sent a text.

"Yeah, I ride for my man.

After spending all day and night together we became inseparable, setting time aside every day to be together, sneaking out at night to stay over at his place."

We seemed to click off jump. We spent most nights cuddled up, just talking about everything and nothing. Soon, we knew each other like the back of our hands, but he seemed to love the street life more than me. I couldn't take the worrying, but what could I do? That came with the territory when you fell for a hustler.

It had been about two weeks, and I hadn't had my period, and I was beginning to get scared. I five-finger discounted a pregnancy test at the local pharmacy. I cut from school and went to my cousin Cakes' crib to take the test. I nearly cried as I saw a plus sign. I was fifteen and pregnant. What was I going to tell my mom?

I put the test in my bag and headed home around three o'clock. As I opened the door, I ran right into my brother, and my whole bag spilled on the floor. I tried to hide the test, but it was too late; he had seen the results.

He was Hella mad, and he wouldn't stop asking questions. After about an hour of fighting, I cracked and told him who the father was. He made a call to one of his people and found out Jacob was at the basketball courts.

I chased him across the park to stop him, but it was too late. My brother hit Jacob with a hard punch to the face and told Jacob my real age. My heart dropped. The next thing I knew, my brother was on the floor, sleeping. I ran home with tears in my eyes.

I sent Jacob a text saying, "I'm sorry about my brother. I'm fifteen, and I'm keeping the baby. I hope you're not mad. We need to talk." The next day, my phone rang, and it was Taylor.

"He had heard that I could sing and wanted to meetup to talk. He had a song for me to sing. After a quick convo, I sang some Keisha Cole, and he was hooked on my voice."

We began to exchange numbers. The next thing I knew, someone walked up in a hood and knocked Taylor out cold. Then he stopped and took off his hood. It was Jacob. He gave me the look of death and walked away. I sat and cried, waiting for Taylor to wake up.

About seven months had passed, and it was time for my baby shower. I had my friend drop a card under Jacob's door, hoping he would come so we could talk everything out. It was 8 pm., and the baby shower was just getting started. The room was packed. All of a sudden, the music stopped.

I turned my head and saw Jacob Walk in. I pushed my brother out of the way and quickly ran to give him a hug and kiss on the cheek. I whispered in his ear that we needed to talk. After some quick convo and apologies, we mingled with the guests.

Out of nowhere, Taylor walked in, he was dressed" like
 he just came out of a music video. I wrapped my arms
around Jacob, praying they wouldn't fight. Taylor shook
 Jacob's hand and gave me a kiss on the cheek.

He handed me an envelope that said here is something
 to get you started on life. Then he just walked out the door
 with a wink and a wave. As I held Jacob's hand, all I felt was
 cold. The next thing I knew, he passed out in my arms.

After what seemed like a lifetime, Jacob woke up
a few minutes later, unaware of what just happened.
About a half-hour later, the party was over.


I walked Jacob home hand in hand, and then my heel
 broke. I almost fell, but Jacob was quick to catch me.
The next thing I knew, Jacob asked if I was okay.

"I miss you; I said as if he read my mind.
 "I miss you too," he replied. Me and Jacob
went up to his place and spent the whole night
talking, watching the sunset and rise.

"After a quick breakfast, he took me home. It had been "about two weeks since me and Jacob moved into our own place, a one-bedroom in the city.

I sat down to rest after a long day of unpacking. I got a knock on the door. I opened it and saw my cousin Katelyn with a face full of tears. She had just had a fight with her man and was afraid to go home, so I told her she could crash here until she got back on her feet.

Jacob and Katelyn clicked right off the bat and decided to go into the drug trade together. Every night, they hit the clubs and moved what they called work to all the rich kids and white-collar bosses. In a few months, if the investment worked out, we would have enough to sit on for a while. We paid four months' rent upfront and bought a bed and a small couch.

I spent most of my nights sitting on it alone, so I made plans to sleep over at my mom's tonight. It had been a while since we spoke,

" I had so many baby "questions to ask her. I was seven months pregnant. I frowned as I looked in the mirror; no wonder Jacob wouldn't bother with me. I left Jacob a note.

I put it on the fridge to let him know where I was, so he wouldn't blow up my phone, "Hey babe, I'm staying at my mom's tonight. See you in the morning.

XoXo, Elise.

The next day, I came home early, and the house was a mess clothes on the floor and dirty dishes in the sink. But what could I do? A woman's work is never done. I walked past Jacob and Katelyn playing Wii bowling. I could swear she rolled her eyes at me. Maybe I was just bugging, but something seemed a little different between them.

Something was going on, but I couldn't figure out what. Call it women's intuition. Three months had passed, and Katelyn barely talked to me anymore.

All she did was sleep, shop, and hit the clubs at night. The next thing I knew, my water broke. My whole body was filled with pain from my first contraction. I called Jacob but got no answer. The pain in my body was too much, so I hit the emergency button on my cell.

I sent Jacob a text, "I'm on my way to the hospital, wish you were here. Elise." The next thing I knew, Jacob walked through the door covered in blood.

He told me Swift had just died in his arms. Jacob walked me down as the ambulance arrived. I told him I would be okay and to shower and change as the ambulance pulled off.

A second contraction came, then a third. At this rate, I was going to have the baby before I ever reached the hospital. After running a couple of red lights, we finally arrived. The ambulance driver quickly rushed me to the labor and delivery room.

"The next thing I "knew, I was being told to breathe. They gave me a mild sedative to slow down my heart rate. I was covered in sweat when Jacob walked in. He looked even more nervous than me, but it was good to have him by my side. After what seemed like a lifetime, with one hard push and a cry, baby Hope was born.

The doctor told me I needed my rest. Jacob left to get a haircut. He wanted to look good for his two angels. It had been two days since I last saw Jacob, and I was starting to worry. Today, the baby was finally coming home.

I called my mom. After an argument, she came and picked me up. I put the baby to sleep as my phone began to ring. It was my cousin Katelyn. She told me Jacob was in the hospital.

She was going to check on him and said she would watch the baby tomorrow for me so I could see him. I called the hospital and found out that Jacob had been admitted to the mental ward."

He was under observation, having had a nervous breakdown, and was being treated for sleep deprivation. Damn, baby, what are we going to do? After a long night of feeding and changing, tomorrow has finally come.

Katelyn is out of my house before eight o'clock. She walks in and gives me a hug as the baby begins to cry. She takes her out of my arms and begins to rock her. Hope smiles and giggles.

As I leave, Katelyn bounces her around and makes funny faces. She is going to make a good mom one day. As I walk out of my building, snow begins to fall. I arrive at the hospital at noon. After getting a visitor's pass, I wait for the elevator for what seems like a lifetime after a quick bag check.

I find Jacob in h i s room, looking out the window at" the snow. I grab him by the hand; his eyes look sad. A doctor walks in, and I sign for some tests. Before I know it, it's time to leave.

The snow has stopped falling. I hop in a cab with no traffic, and I'm home in a matter of minutes. I walk through the house; all I hear is silence, something I haven't heard in days.

Katelyn moved out but comes to visit every day and watch Hope so I can see Jacob. Today's a good day. Jacob has finally been released from the hospital and looks like the man I had fallen in love with. Hope is asleep in her room. I call Katelyn but get no answer.

I open the bathroom door and see her on the floor holding a birth control test in her hands. I take the test from her hands and ask her who's the lucky man.

She pushes me against the wall, runs out of the room holding the test, and throws it at Jacob, who runs out "of the apartment behind her.

I can't believe my eyes. I guess I was right.

As I turn to pack up Jacob's things, I hear a gunshot followed by sirens and a knock on the door. The cops tell me that Jacob has been killed while running out of the building, a case of mistaken identity.

**"when something feels right, it can't be wrong. When you fall in love, it's like a song, and you never know what you've got till it's gone" Forever.**

# CHAPTER 4

## Fearless/Swift

*"life is short. Live life to the fullest. Treat every day like it's your last cause, it just might be."*

My name's Jason, but everybody calls me Swift because I make fast moves. I've just been shot, and my life's flashing before my eyes.

Mom always said that street life only leads you to two places: dead or in jail. Let's start at the beginning. The day started the same as every other day has for the last few years. I woke up around twelve, took a shower, got fly, and hit the block to hustle. Me and my team had saved up some paper and were looking to take over. The only thing in our way was another hustler named Ledgend, who knew the streets and was far from stupid.

Well, if you can't beat them, join them.

After about a week of searching, I saw Ledgend posted up on a mailbox on the strip, hand on a hammer. I approached him slowly. I threw my cousin Gunz's name in the air before he could speak. I gassed his head up, and he put me and my people down under him. We shared a fifty- fifty split of all profits, and everything came through him and his connection.

In a few days, we set up shop on a small strip by Columbia. Me, my dude Franklin, and Ace set up a twenty-four-hour spot, each taking shifts. After a few days, word got around, and paper started coming in from all directions. The first of the month came, and I paid Ledgend his percentage and split my half with my clique. Ledgend barely came by; he had fallen for a shorty, and they spent most of their days together. I don't blame him. She was the wifey type, small, smart, with a body for days.

"Word around the "street" was she was only fifteen. You know what they say better him than me. I walked out of my crib for the night shift. As snow slowly began to fall, I stood in the hallway. After about two hours, I called it a night. It was about three in the morning when I walked about a block and saw a dude posted up making sales. I pulled out my hammer.

Before he could turn his head, I pistol-whipped him. It was about thirty below, but the anger in me had me feeling warm. I kicked the dude in the ribs, put the hammer in his mouth, and said, "This is my block, get off it. The next time I see you here, I'm not going to be so nice." I kicked him in the ribs a few more times for good measure and headed home.

Even with the round-the-clock system me and my crew had setup, there was still competition over territory. I wanted in on every block. If a nickel bag was getting sold in the park, I wanted in. I was starting to sound like Frank White. It's good to be king, but everybody wanted to take your place.

"I made moves while "Ledgend" became more of a silent partner and moved to the city to expand, making stops now and then to get his paper.

Ever since the fight over territory things hadn't been the same. It was getting to the point that I had to walk strapped at all times. One afternoon, I got a call from Ace that there was a problem on the block. Franklin had just been pressed by some local Bloods and had been jumped. This was something we couldn't let go of. We waited about a week and let the tension die down.

I hit up my cousin Gunz and got two. Thirty-Eight pistols and a sawed-off shotgun. We head to the block; it's time to start a war. I run up on Fame, the guy who pressed Franklin on the corner.

I hit him once in the chest with the double barrel. Ace and Franklin take care of his other two goons, shooting one in the hand and the other in the kneecap.

"We get the job done in a matter of minutes and rob "them to make it look like a stick-up gone wrong. The next day, we setup shop like nothing ever happened. I can't help but feel like a boss.

I wake up early and hit up my dude Reyes to get a new tattoo on my hand a dollar sign with horns and a tail letting me know that money's the root of all evil. I must be the devil because money is coming in from everywhere. My whole team's looking flashy.

Gucci this, Louie that, gun belt with shades to match. I turn and get a call from Ledgend. He says he wants to meet up in front of the mailbox where we first met. As I Walk, it begins to snow outside. Damn, I'm going to fuck up my new shoes. It's time to put an end to Ledgend and take over.

"As he walks up, I feel guilty, but it's too late to care now. I reach in for a pound. I can't help but feel on edge. I wonder if he predicted my moves. The next thing I know, I hear the screech of tires. A van pulls up." Four goons hop out and start to fire. Ledgend pulls his hammer, unaware of what's going on. I turn, but it's too late. I'm hit. The van speeds off as I slowly slip away in the arms of the man I was planning to kill.

**" Time is short. Live every day as if it's your last. Always do right by the people who help you because you never know when it's going to be all over."**

# CHAPTER 5

## Heartless/Gunz

**"Sometimes loss makes you do crazy things, anger blurs the lines between right and wrong and you realize it's more about the point than the principal."**

My name's Abraham, but everyone calls me Gunz because I'm a shooter. Everyone deserves a shot. I knew that Taylor had nothing to do with Swift's death, but in a way, I held him responsible. Glorifying a lifestyle, he knows nothing about, lying to the youth, making selling drugs and disrespectful behavior seem acceptable.

It's all about the sneakers, flashing bread, and fucking bitches like none of us grew up with little sisters. Feeding everyone an image and a pipe dream.

"When Jacob called me and said Taylor had the nerve" to threaten him and our lifestyle, I had enough. I asked around and found out that Taylor" had a show in the Tunnel. I knew what had to be done.

Ledgend felt guilty and wanted to make things right. I told him to dress in a black sweatsuit and meet me in front of the mailbox in front of Swift's crib.

Tonight, after his performance, we set a trap. Cakes would sit at the bar, flirt with Taylor, and fill his head with hopes of sex in the bathroom, feeding his ego every man's dream.

We arrived at the Tunnel around ten. The club was packed, standing room only. Taylor sang a few love songs and his new single "Man Down." Kind of ironic.

"After signing a few autographs and the chest of a couple of groupies, Taylor headed to the bar where Cakes was waiting, dressed to kill. I missed hitting that; maybe if I was more grown, I would have made "her wifey.

Tonight, we had no time to play catch-up. After about half an hour, Cakes sent me a text with a sheep emoji telling me that the lamb was ready for the slaughter.

The roofie kicked in, and Taylor started stumbling. Cakes was holding his hand and guiding him to the bathroom stall. As he walked in, Taylor saw me waiting, holding a hammer and realized that he had been set up. He punched Cakes in the face, and she stumbled backward into the stall next door. I pistol whipped him, and he started bleeding from his nose.

Ledgend lost it and took him into the stall, beating him until he was limp. I pulled him off of Taylor and fired two shots into his chest.

"I grabbed Cakes by the hand and pulled the fire alarm on the way out of the club. with all of panic I lost cakes in the crowd" after "pushing through the club, I ended up outside. I saw "Cakes get in a cab with Ledgend and run down the block to the sound of sirens from both ambulances and cop cars.

A few days later, Ledgend met up with me in front of Swift's building and handed me a book bag full of money and drugs. He told me he was getting out of the life to raise his daughter.

I took the money and handed the drugs to Franklin and Ace and did the same. The next day I went to Los crib to smoke a blunt I walked in, and franklin and ace were sitting on the couch getting some work cut after rolling up I put a lighter too the best joint I ever rolled before I could take a pull the door was broken down next thing, I knew I was back in jail.

**"Loss will make you do crazy things and make decisions without thinking. Anger can turn you into a killer if you let it, and it can make you look at life differently and change your whole perspective."**

# CHAPTER 6

## Reckless/Taylor

*"All my life I have always been a dream chaser. I always wanted to be rich and famous, and fame is a powerful drug that no rehab can cure."*

Looking back at my childhood, it feels like a series of life defining events. I lost my mom when I was about ten years old. She was walking home from buying me a cake for my birthday when a drunk driver lost control of their car and jumped the sidewalk, hitting her and killing her instantly.

My mom was the kindest, most loving woman I ever met. Before bed every night, she always told me, "Good night, dream big baby, one day you're going to be a star." After my mom's death, I went into a shell and mostly stood alone. My dad was around, but he was going through things himself, trying to keep a roof over the heads of two young children while dealing with my mom's passing. He held on to a bottle, drinking until he passed out, waking up hoping time would reset.

I escaped reality in a different way, locked in my room with my headphones, listening to hip-hop mixtapes. One day, the battery died o n my Walkman. The song I was listening to cut off mid-verse. I started to rap as if the song was my own version. I later found out this was called free styling, and from that moment on, I wanted to become a rapper.

I picked up a couple of tapes of Jay-Z instrumentals, and I was hooked. I bought a notebook and started writing songs. I guess you could say music was my first love. I soon started recording singles of my own in a small studio in one of my friend's houses. In a few weeks, I finished my first mixtape called Hood Dreams. The mixtape did okay, and I soon became hood famous.

People would stop me on the street, saying they liked my music, and all the girls wanted to be my wife. I soon fell in love with a girl named Nicole. She was bad and had the voice of an angel but couldn't write music. We fell into friendship and then love. She was the reason I wrote my first love song, "I'm So in Love." It was my first hit record.

It's amazing how good "Pussy" will motivate you to create beautiful things. After generating an Internet buzz, I got asked to be a guest on DJ Slays hip-hop show. I was scared to death to appear, but my mom always told me to dream big, so I showed up.

After a quick interview, talking flashy, and playing my songs, the show was about to end. But before I had to go, the host asked me to freestyle. He put on the instrumental "Feel it in the Air," and I went off, "I got three guns way bigger than Rerun, hydro got my eyes low, it's so hard to see from them.

Them Jewels is nice, how 'bout you run them? Sick the way I son men like their wifey when she hasn't seen her one   friend. Yeah, you know the one friend, all upset shit should have known better than to go in unprotected, the streets are reckless."

The DJ lost his mind and gave me a cosign, "You're listening to Taylor; this kid is a problem." Within a year, I was signed to a major label. Nicole and I broke up, and I was lost without her. Instead of being sad, I let all my pain out on a record called "Tears on Her Pillow."

Every record I dropped was a hit. I soon started a world tour. Lately, I haven't been inspired. I can't write a song  to save my life. Then I got a phone call that my dad passed away from a heart attack in his sleep.

After the funeral, I went to his old place to meet with  my sister Angela to catch up and look at old pictures. With all the touring,

I hadn't seen my sister in over two years. As I walked to my dad's house, I heard someone singing Keisha Cole. She had a voice that made me walk faster. I had to know where this sound was coming from; she drew me towards her like a siren.

I turned my head and saw a beautiful woman sitting on the steps of her building, looking sad with her head down, singing. I walked up, and she jumped up like she saw a ghost, fumbling her words. "You're Taylor! I have all your music. I'm your biggest fan."

I responded, "I heard your voice, and I had to meet you. I guess you could say I'm your biggest fan, beautiful. My bad, love, just got lost in your eyes." They were a mix of blue and green, the way the light hit them was mesmerizing. I caught myself. "Let's try this again. My name's Taylor. What's your name, love?"

She said, "My name's Elise, but I don't mind being called
 love, as long as you don't mind. "Sounds good, love. I think
we can make beautiful music together. I handed her my phone
 to give her my number.

I felt someone tap me on the shoulder. I turned around and
got hit with a roundhouse punch to the jaw. I woke up forty
minutes later with Elise  holding me, tears in her eyes. I
looked up and said, "I'm okay, love, no need to cry. Before
we were  rudely interrupted, I was trying to get your number.

"She replied, "I put it in your phone."

I gave her a quick hug and said, "I'll call you later." I went
to my dad's old apartment, had lunch, and  put some Ice on
my face. The whole time, I couldn't get Elise  off my  mind.
A  nigga  needs  to  know what you're feeling inside.

"Out of nowhere, I wrote my next big record after looking through old photos and telling stories. I called my driver and told him to take me to the Checkers drive thru and then the studio. I dropped three tracks back- t o - b a c k and named the project I do This for You in memory of my mother and my inspiration, Elise.

A few days later, I called Elise. After a few rings, she picked up, sounding sad. She told me she'd been going through some things. I asked her if she wanted to record. After some small talk and pleading, she agreed.

I dropped by her building in my white Escalade and got out to help her in. She was dressed in a pair of ripped jeans and a tight-fitting T-shirt from my tour three years ago. "I told you I was your biggest fan." Elise seemed stressed. I told her we were going to be recording for a couple of hours, so we might as well pick up some food and drinks.

I asked her what she would like to eat She said, "General Tso's chicken wings with fries "crispy. A woman who knows what she wants to eat honestly, I'm impressed. I ordered General Tso's wings, extra spicy with pork fried rice, and some egg rolls for later. The guy threw in a few fortune cookies on the house.

I took her to my home studio so we could escape all the distractions of the world. We arrived around 10 o'clock and sat down, listening to a few beats I had set aside. Elise couldn't seem to find her groove.

I asked if she was okay. She told me she been having boyfriend problems and was sorry for wasting my time and for the incident with Jacob. I told her it was cool, no hard feelings. I hoped he learned to treat her better, or I might have to take her away from him. She smiled and turned red. "Good to see you smile, love." I put on my new album, and we had a listening party, sitting on the studio sofa, eating wings.

She listened closely to my every word. I reached out, held her hand, and leaned in to kiss her. After a short pause, she kissed me back, and we started making out while lying down. Things started to get heavy. She sat up. and said,

"You know I got a man. "I responded, "I got goldfish," and pointed to a tank full of koi fish against the wall. As She giggled.

I leaned in for a second kiss, and she stopped again and said, "I wanted to have this moment with you forever. Not every girl gets to live out all of her fantasies with her music crush." guess I'm lucky.

Mid-sentence, I said, "You're also smart, funny, and beautiful. Let's live in the moment. You set the pace, love." Elise stood up and took off her t-shirt, then slowly unbuttoned her jeans. They hit the floor. I held her hand so she wouldn't fall as she stepped out of them.

She took off her bra and panties. I stood up, and she said, "Sit down," then opened my jeans, pulled out my manhood, and guided it inside her. She took half of it inside and paused, then began to ride me slowly at first, taking short breaths between moans. I grabbed her by the hip and put my other hand on her neck, enough pressure to make her skip a breath but not enough to hurt her.

Elise began to pick up pace. I leaned back against the wall, letting her use me as her personal stress relief. After ten minutes, we came together. She slowed down, kept riding me until I got hard again, and then got up and lay down on her stomach.

I lined up and started hitting it from behind. Her moans motivated me to go harder and faster. In one deep thrust, it was all over. We went upstairs and took a shower together, letting the water run down our bodies. We went downstairs, changed, and fell asleep on the sofa.

The next day, I dropped Elise home around eight in the morning. She sent me a text around noon, saying, "Thank you for the amazing night, but we can't do this anymore.

I still love my ex, Jacob."

The next day, I went to Japan, the first stop on my world tour. For six months, I worked nonstop. I came back to the States and ordered General Tso's wings. I sent Elise a text: "How you been, love? Just got back off tour." She told me she was doing okay and that she was having a baby shower at the church hall on Richards Street. If I had time, she said, I should pop up.

I got a fresh cut and put ten thousand in hundreds in a white envelope. I arrived at the party at random, gave Elise a hug, put the money in her purse, and shook her boyfriend's hand. I whispered in his ear, "Be careful."

"A few days later, I drove to see my sister and ran into Jacob at an intersection. While waiting for the stoplight to change, I rolled down the window with a forty Cal on my lap, planning to scare him. I was about to say, "You better treat her right."

Before I could speak, the cops pulled up next to me. I tucked the gun in my hoodie. The light turned green. Jacob shot me a dirty look and went into the train station.

About a week later, I had an album release party at the Tunnel. The crowd lost their minds; everybody knew all my songs. I paused while the crowd finished my sentences. The rush was unbelievable. "Mom, I finally made it. Your boy's a star."

I headed to the bar to get a cold drink. The stage light made me feel tired. A beautiful girl with curls and a body for days offered to buy me a drink. I ordered a Henny and coke After thirty minutes of flirting, shorty grabbed me by the hand to lead me to the bathroom.

"My lucky night I was "about to get some groupie love. "The door closed behind us. A couple of goons were waiting for me, dressed all in black. I tried to push past them, hitting Shorty by mistake and knocking her down. I turned and got hit in the face with the handle of a Smith & Wesson. A second guy rushed me and beat me to the point I couldn't stand. They both grabbed me and threw me into the corner stall. They pointed guns at me and fired two shots.

I started to breathe heavily and passed out, listening to the screams of my fans. I woke up in a hospital room a few days later. The doctor told me I was a lucky guy; the bullets didn't hit any major arteries, and in a few weeks with some rest, I should make a full recovery.

"They say fame is a powerful drug, and ego can get the best of you. Money can make you feel invincible. When life starts to move fast, you start to act reckless. It sometimes takes a bullet to slow you down."

# CHAPTER 7

## They Grow Up Too Fast

It's funny how time flies. It feels like only yesterday I fell in love, lost the love of my life, and then gave birth to a baby girl who became my reason for living. My heart kept me strong and taught me to believe that anything  is possible.

So, I named her Hope.

I still remember the first day of school. Hope was so excited that she stayed up the whole night with me, asking questions until she fell asleep on the sofa. When it was time to drop her off at school, she gave me one of those "never let me go" hugs.

Now, she is starting her first day of high school. They grow up too fast.

# CHAPTER 8

## Like Looking in A Mirror

It's been years since the love of my life was taken away from me. I didn't even get to say goodbye. It's funny how fast time passes. I lost everyone in my life that I ever loved. Me and my cousin Elise haven't spoken in years, but I am not mad at her. Never thought I would ever have a reason to love again.

That changed the day I gave birth to my baby girl. She became my reason to smile, wake up, and change my life. That's why I named her Faith. The way she talks, laughs, and even smiles reminds me of Jacob. It's just like looking in the mirror sometimes.

# CHAPTER 9

## Hope/Speechless

**"Never been the type to believe in love at first sight until you meet someone that makes you lose your focus."**

It's the first day of school, and I'm already late. Great way to make a first impression. I just ran for the bus and I'm out of breath. I put on my headphones to zone out the morning noise of crying kids and the weekend gossip from a woman who doesn't seem to know how to control the sound of her voice.

As I turn to take a seat, my pocket vibrates. It's a text from my mom: "Have a great day, baby." I respond with a smiley face. I love my mom, but sometimes she gets on my nerves. "After about four stops and a quick walk, I finally "made it to school. I'm late, but since it's the first day, they let it slide."

They ask for my name, give me a program, and tell me my first class is English. It's also my homeroom, so at least I can kill two birds with one stone. I run through the halls, hoping to beat the bell. Just my luck, I trip on my shoelace but don't fall someone catches me before I hit the ground.

I look up and think I'm dreaming. For the first time in my life, I am speechless. While I stand there, he introduces himself. "I'm James. Are you okay, love?" I reply with a quick head nod. As I walk away, he asks my name. I say, "Hope." He smiles and says, "See you around, love." I think I'm going to like this school. As I walk to my homeroom, I see a circle of chairs with one spot open.

"I take a seat next to a girl with the greenest eyes I've ever seen. Our homeroom teacher introduces herself. "Hello, everyone. My name is Ms. Boyhend, but feel free to call me Lyn. Today, we are going to get to" know each other better." We pass around a ball and say our names. I say, "Hope," and pass the ball to the girl next to me with the greenest eyes I ever seen. She says, "Hello, everybody. My name is Faith."

The whole class laughs. Faith and I hit it off right away and have all the same classes, so we spent the day getting to know each other. She's kind of wild but a cool girl. As we walk through the hall, I see James my future husband. Faith bolts to him and gives him a big hug and a kiss on the cheek. Faith introduces me as her new friend, Hope.

James replies, "Long time no see."

"I ask Faith if she knows James. She says they  met over the summer; he just moved to New York from Florida. "He's fly, right?" I turn red and  change the subject. I get to my next class just in "time before the bell rings, I see James at lunch  and take a seat right next to him.

After some small talk I ask if he and faith are seeing each other he says were just homies. I would like to get to  know you better." We exchange numbers just as Faith walks  up to us and takes a seat right  between me  and James.

# CHAPTER 10

## One Hot Summer

**"when you fall in love It feels like you have been hit with a brick more like a gunshot."**

It's been a Hot Summer. The news says it's eighty-five degrees outside but feels like a hundred. I want to go to the pool, but all my girls are away for summer vacation. I put on my bathing suit and a pair of shorts, hoping the sprinklers are on in front of my building. I hear water as I walk through the lobby and start to run like a fat kid who heard the ice cream truck. As I turned the corner, I hit someone and ended up on my back.

Before I can get up and say something, a guy with the most sexual eyes I've ever seen reaches out a hand to help me up and says, "You got to be careful, love."

I say, "How am I going to be your love if I don't know your name?" He smiles and says, "My name's James. I just moved here a week ago. Where are you rushing off to?"

I tell him, "I'm going to the pool. You want to be my swimming buddy? He responds, "How can I be your swimming buddy if I don't know your name? "After a quick pause, I introduce myself.

After picking up some swim trunks from his crib, we head to the pool. We split up on the way into the changing rooms. I can't wait to see him with his shirt off.

After a quick walk, I see James waiting for me, sitting poolside with his feet in the water. I make a quick turn and ask, "What do you think?"

Without a pause, he says, "You're beautiful," and for the first time in my life, I believe it. I play off being impressed and push him into the pool, then jump in after him and hit him with a big splash of water. He responds, "So, you want to play rough?" Then he does something that surprises me to this day. He leans in and pinches my nose, and says, "Tag, you're it."

I reply, "I'm on base," and jump into his arms. Something about the way he holds me makes me feel so safe. The way he looks into my eyes makes me feel like the only one in the world.

**To be continued...**

**in Sleepless Volume II: A Different Time.**

# ABOUT THE AUTHOR

Eric Murphy is a music artist and author from Red Hook, Brooklyn, known in the industry as the Pseudonym Ledgend. Renowned for ghostwriting hit records, he started writing "Sleepless Over Time," a project he created to tell the story of the ups and downs of urban life. This love story is told through the perspective of a colorful cast of characters, giving a personal feel to the urban romance novel genre. Set in the early nineties, it paints a vivid picture of life in New York City.

Milton Keynes UK
Ingram Content Group UK Ltd.
UKHW020114181024
449757UK00012B/813

9 798330 380671